Dear Parents and Educators,

Welcome to Penguin Young Readers! As parents and educators, you
know that each child develops at his or her own pace—in terms of
speech, critical thinking, and, of course, reading. Penguin Young
Readers recognizes this fact. As a result, each Penguin Young Readers
book is assigned a traditional easy-to-read level (1–4) as well as a
Guided Reading Level (A–P). Both of these systems will help you choose
the right book for your child. Please refer to the back of each book
for specific leveling information. Penguin Young Readers features
esteemed authors and illustrators, stories about favorite characters,
fascinating nonfiction, and more!

Shape Spotters

LEVEL 2

GUIDED
READING
LEVEL **E**

This book is perfect for a **Progressing Reader** who:
- can figure out unknown words by using picture and context clues;
- can recognize beginning, middle, and ending sounds;
- can make and confirm predictions about what will happen in the text; and
- can distinguish between fiction and nonfiction.

Here are some **activities** you can do during and after reading this book:
- Make Connections: Ms. Carey's students are able to find lots of different
  shapes in their school. Think about your classroom at school. What
  shapes can you find there?
- Picture Clues: Many beginning readers use picture clues to help them
  figure out the meaning of words. Reread this book and point to the
  pictures of shapes and the corresponding words. On a separate sheet
  of paper, draw and label all the shapes mentioned in the book.

Remember, sharing the love of reading with a child is the best gift
you can give!

—Bonnie Bader, EdM
  Penguin Young Readers program

*Penguin Young Readers are leveled by independent reviewers applying the standards developed by Irene Fountas
and Gay Su Pinnell in *Matching Books to Readers: Using Leveled Books in Guided Reading*, Heinemann, 1999.

For the *real* Dan, Kate, Ann,
Pete, and Mike, with love—MEB

For Mom and Pops, with love—SS

Penguin Young Readers
Published by the Penguin Group
Penguin Group (USA) Inc., 375 Hudson Street, New York, New York 10014, USA
Penguin Group (Canada), 90 Eglinton Avenue East, Suite 700, Toronto, Ontario M4P 2Y3, Canada
(a division of Pearson Penguin Canada Inc.)
Penguin Books Ltd., 80 Strand, London WC2R 0RL, England
Penguin Group Ireland, 25 St. Stephen's Green, Dublin 2, Ireland (a division of Penguin Books Ltd.)
Penguin Group (Australia), 250 Camberwell Road, Camberwell, Victoria 3124, Australia
(a division of Pearson Australia Group Pty. Ltd.)
Penguin Books India Pvt. Ltd., 11 Community Centre, Panchsheel Park, New Delhi—110 017, India
Penguin Group (NZ), 67 Apollo Drive, Rosedale, Auckland 0632, New Zealand
(a division of Pearson New Zealand Ltd.)
Penguin Books (South Africa) (Pty.) Ltd., 24 Sturdee Avenue,
Rosebank, Johannesburg 2196, South Africa

Penguin Books Ltd., Registered Offices: 80 Strand, London WC2R 0RL, England

Text copyright © 2002 by Penguin Group (USA) Inc. Illustrations copyright © 2002 by Sami Sweeten.
All rights reserved. First published in 2002 by Grosset & Dunlap, an imprint of Penguin Group (USA) Inc.
Published in 2012 by Penguin Young Readers, an imprint of Penguin Group (USA) Inc.,
345 Hudson Street, New York, New York 10014. Manufactured in China.

Library of Congress Control Number: 2002004655

ISBN 978-0-448-42858-1   10 9 8 7 6 5 4 3 2 1

SHAPE SPOTTERS

by Megan E. Bryant
illustrated by Sami Sweeten

Penguin Young Readers
An Imprint of Penguin Group (USA) Inc.

Ms. Carey's class is hunting

for shapes.

They hunt for a shape
in the library.

6

The shape has four sides.

It is not a square.

Look around you.

It's everywhere!

Dan sees some books.

The books are rectangles.

A rectangle has four sides.

It is not square.

All the kids pick up rectangles.

They hunt for a shape
in the music room.

The shape has three sides.

Hear it ring.

It is not a bell.

But it goes

ping, ping, ping.

Kate sees a triangle.

It has three sides.

It goes **ping**, **ping**, **ping**.

All the kids get triangles.

All the kids go

ping, ping, ping.

They hunt for a shape outside.

The shape has no beginning.

The shape has no end.

It goes around and around.

It curves and it bends.

Ann sees some hoops.

The hoops are circles.

A circle has no beginning.

It has no end.

It goes around and around.

All the kids play with circles.

They hunt for a shape

in the lunchroom.

The shape has four sides,

all exactly the same.

It's not a rectangle.

Do you know its name?

Pete sees some

sandwiches.

The sandwiches

are squares.

A square has
four sides.
All four sides
are the same.

21

Ms. Carey says,

"Watch this."

Look! Two rectangles.

Look! Two triangles.

All the kids eat

squares, rectangles,

and triangles for lunch.

They hunt for a shape
in the art room.

The shape is not a square.

The shape is not a rectangle.

It has four sides.

It is turned on an angle.

Mike sees some cutouts.

The cutouts are diamonds.

A diamond has four sides.

It is not a square

or a rectangle.

All the kids make pictures
with the diamonds.

The bell rings.

It is time to go home.

Wait! There is one more shape!

It is a star.

All the kids get stars.

Ms. Carey says,

"Great work, shape spotters!

See you tomorrow."

31

Did you find all the shapes?

There are more.

Go back and look

for the hidden shapes

in the pictures!